Chilly
Saves the Day

The story of Chilly Saves the Day
and all the pictures in this book are
original and have been specially
commissioned for Tesco.

Published for
Tesco Stores Limited
by Brilliant Books Ltd
84-86 Regent Street
London W1B 5RR

First published 2000

Text and Illustrations © 2000 Brilliant Books Ltd
Printed by Printer Trento S.r.l., Italy
Reproduction by Graphic Ideas Studios, England
ISBN 1-84221-128-5

1 3 5 7 9 10 8 6 4 2

fun to learn

collection

Chilly
Saves the Day

Written by Katie Trimmer
Illustrated by Claire Tindall

Chilly the snowman was a magical snowman who lived at the North Pole with Father Christmas, Mother Christmas and all the elves.

Ever since he'd come to life, one
snowy Christmas Eve, he'd settled in
nicely with Father Christmas's family.
    He helped the little elves with their
woodwork and he made sure all his animal
friends had plenty of fresh vegetables
and hay to eat. And now, he'd even been
allowed to help out with the Winter Festival,
which went on for two whole days.

Apart from Christmas itself,
the Winter Festival was
the highlight of the year,
but there was a lot to do.

The lake had to be
swept clean for the
skating competition.

The skis and sledges
had to be brought down
from Father Christmas's loft
and Mother Christmas had to
get her team of elves fit for the
great tug-of-war competition.

FINISH

It seemed ages before
everything was ready and
when the first day of the
festival finally arrived, all
the elves chattered excitedly
and some of the littlest ones
clung to Mother Christmas's skirts.

The first event of the day was the ski race. Raffles the reindeer saw himself as winning material, but he knew there was some stiff competition. Eric the elf had been in training all year. Chilly blew his whistle and they were off as fast as their skis would carry them.

Skier after skier came racing round the corner and disappeared over the edge and landed in a big heap. Someone had changed the route of the ski race!

The crowd gasped – surely that wasn't the way the ski race was meant to go!

The next event was the tug-of-war. This was the moment Mother Christmas had been waiting for all year. There had never been a Winter Festival when her team hadn't won.

"Good luck," whispered Chilly before raising his hankie over his head.
"Ready, steady, go!" he yelled...
The two teams pulled up the slack and heaved with all their might.

The elves pulled hard and the animals found themselves being dragged forwards towards the middle line.

"Hang on!"
Raffles the reindeer shouted as they edged towards the middle line. And then...PIONNG!
The rope snapped in two!

The final event of the day was the ice-sculpting competition. Out in the valley beside the frozen lake the elves and animals had been working all week at making the perfect sculptures.

But when the competitors stood by their
work and proudly pulled off the covers,
something was terribly wrong.
One of the little elves burst into tears.
"I didn't do it like that, honestly," he sobbed.
"No dear," Mother Christmas said grimly,
"but we're going to find out who did!"

Chilly found his friend, Raffles the reindeer.
"We've got to find out who's behind all this
naughtiness before the second day of the festival
is ruined too," he said. "Yes," said Raffles, "but how?"
"Well," said Chilly, "I think we should lay
a trap! But we'll have to be quick."

Raffles and Chilly headed over to the big barn where the snowballs were stored ready for the snowball throwing contest the next day.
They dug a big hole, then they waited nervously in the silence. Chilly heard a sound. "Shh," he whispered to Raffles. "I think someone's coming."

Slowly a dark shape shuffled towards them. Raffles and Chilly held their breath.

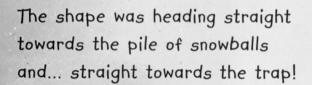

The shape was heading straight towards the pile of snowballs and... straight towards the trap!

Chilly gripped Raffles' arm. There was a yell in the dark, followed by a large crash! "We've got him!" Chilly cried. "Light the lantern, Raffles!"

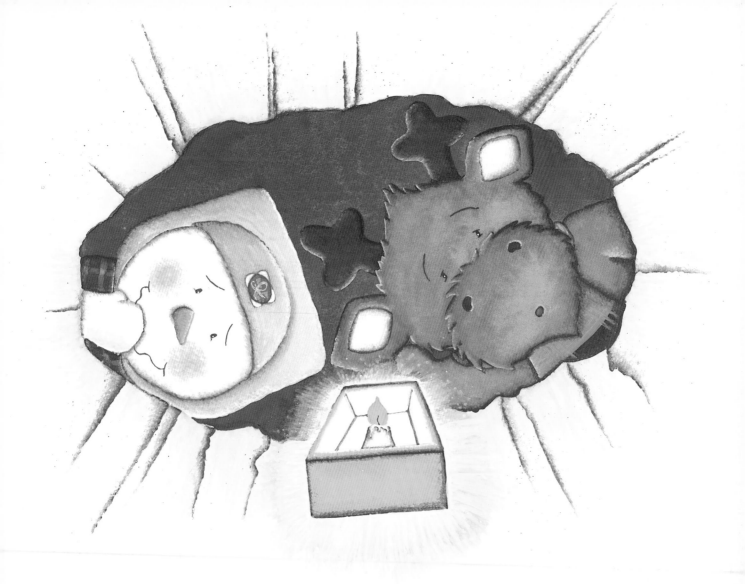

"Get me out of here now!" came a very cross voice.
"Not until you explain yourself," Chilly said bravely.
"It's you who've got some explaining to do!" said the
voice. "I was doing my rounds and the next thing
I know, I'm down this hole!" Chilly gulped - they'd
trapped Norman by mistake! The chief elf!

It took Norman quite some time to calm down.
"I'll thank you not to take the law into your
own hands in future. Now you're both to go
straight to bed!" he said crossly.

"Yes, sir. Sorry, sir," Chilly and Raffles said
together for about the tenth time. They'd never
known anyone get quite as cross as Norman.

After a terrible night of tossing and turning,
Chilly woke very early, much earlier than everyone
else, and he decided to go for a little walk to
see if he could clear his head. He had just come
into a snowy clearing, when he heard
the sound of distant voices.

"...I can't wait to *see* their faces when their *sledges* fall apart..."
Chilly froze to the spot.
He'd found the culprits!

The laughing voices came closer. Chilly stayed perfectly still, like an ordinary frozen snowman, as two little mooses wandered over towards him.

"What an ugly snowman," one of them said, as they came closer. Chilly waited until they were right in front of him and then said "Boo!" At the same time he grabbed the two mooses by their antlers and tied his scarf around them. "I'm Chilly," said Chilly, "and you're in trouble!"

Everybody was cross
with the naughty mooses.

"What have you got to say for yourselves?"
asked Father Christmas sternly. "Sorry," mumbled Maurice.
"Sorry," mumbled Malcolm. "We just wanted to join in,"
he sniffed. "We know we've been naughty, but if you
just give us a chance, we promise we'll make it up to you."

"Well," said Father Christmas,
"you do seem sorry for what you've done."
"I've got an idea," said Chilly. "They can
hold the finishing line." And do you know
what? They were so well-behaved, that
they were even allowed to go to
the Great Festival Feast.

And they were as good as gold... Or were they?!